D0489947

Note to parents, carers and teachers

Read it yourself is a series of modern stories, favourite characters and traditional tales written in a simple way for children who are learning to read. The books can be read independently or as part of a guided reading session.

Each book is carefully structured to include many high-frequency words vital for first reading. The sentences on each page are supported closely by pictures to help with understanding, and to offer lively details to talk about.

The books are graded into four levels that progressively introduce wider vocabulary and longer stories as a reader's ability and confidence grows.

Ideas for use

- Begin by looking through the book and talking about the pictures. Has your child heard this story before?

- Help your child with any words he does not know, either by helping him to sound them out or supplying them yourself.

- Developing readers can be concentrating so hard on the words that they sometimes don't fully grasp the meaning of what they're reading. Answering the puzzle questions on pages 30 and 31 will help with understanding.

For more information and advice on Read it yourself and book banding, visit **www.ladybird.com/readityourself**

Book
Band
5

Level 1 is ideal for children who have received some initial reading instruction. Each story is told very simply, using a small number of frequently repeated words.

Special features:

Opening pages introduce key story words

flying dinosaurs

teeth

little dinosaurs

Rex

Careful match between story and pictures

Rex was a big dinosaur.
He saw the little dinosaurs.
They were playing.

"Can I play, too?" said Rex.

"Yes," said the little dinosaurs.
"You can play with us."

Large, clear type

Educational Consultant: Geraldine Taylor
Book Banding Consultant: Kate Ruttle

A catalogue record for this book is available from the British Library

Published by Ladybird Books Ltd
80 Strand, London, WC2R 0RL
A Penguin Company

006

ISBN: 978-0-71819-463-5

Printed in China

Rex the
Big Dinosaur

Written by Ronne Randall
Illustrated by Kim Geyer

flying dinosaurs

little dinosaurs

teeth

Rex

7

Rex was a big dinosaur.
He saw the little dinosaurs.
They were playing.

"Can I play, too?" said Rex.

"Yes," said the little dinosaurs.
"You can play with us."

Rex ran after the little dinosaurs. He snapped his big teeth.

The little dinosaurs were scared. They ran away.

Rex saw the little dinosaurs again. They were playing.

"Can I play, too?" said Rex.

"Yes," said the little dinosaurs. "You can play with us."

Rex roared. It was
a very loud roar!

The little dinosaurs were
scared. They ran away.

Rex saw the little
dinosaurs again.

"Can I play with you?"
he said to them.

"No," said the little dinosaurs. "You are too big. You snap your teeth. Your roar is very loud. We are too scared!"

"Go away," said the little dinosaurs.

Rex went away. He was not happy.

21

Then Rex saw some big flying dinosaurs. They scared the little dinosaurs.

23

Rex ran after them.
He roared and he snapped
his teeth.

The flying dinosaurs were
scared and they went away.

The little dinosaurs
were happy.

"Play with us again, Rex!"
they said.

Rex did not roar and he did not snap his big teeth.

The little dinosaurs were happy and so was Rex.

How much do you remember about
the story of Rex the Big Dinosaur?
Answer these questions and find out!

- **Who does Rex want
  to play with?**

- **Why do the little
  dinosaurs tell Rex
  to go away?**

- **How does Rex scare
  the flying dinosaurs?**

Look at the pictures from the story and say the order they should go in.

A

B

C

D

Answer: B, A, D, C.

Read it yourself with Ladybird

Tick the books you've read!

For children who are ready to take their first steps in reading.

Level 1

 The Enormous Turnip ☐

 Fairy Friends ☐

 Goldilocks and the Three Bears ☐

 Little Red Hen ☐

 The Magic Porridge Pot ☐

 Little Creatures ☐

 Recycling Fun! ☐

 The Princess and the Pea ☐

 Cinderella ☐

 Rex the Big Dinosaur ☐

 The Tale of Peter Rabbit ☐

 The Three Billy Goats Gruff ☐

 Why Giraffe has a Long Neck ☐

 Topsy and Tim Go to the Zoo ☐

 The Ugly Duckling ☐

 The Emperor's New Clothes ☐

For beginner readers who can read short, simple sentences with help.

Level 2

 Beauty and the Beast ☐

 Chicken Licken ☐

 Little Red Riding Hood ☐

 Nature Trail ☐

 Sports Day ☐

 Pirate School ☐

 Rumpelstiltskin ☐

 Sleeping Beauty ☐

 The Gingerbread Man ☐

 Sly Fox and Red Hen ☐

 The Tale of Jemima Puddle-Duck ☐

 The Three Little Pigs ☐

 Why Lion Roarrrs! ☐

 Topsy and Tim The Big Race ☐

 Town Mouse Country Mouse ☐

 Dean's Dragon ☐

Available on the App Store

The Read it yourself with Ladybird app is now available for iPad, iPhone and iPod touch

App also available on Android devices